Scholast

A READING GUIDE TO

Bridge to Terabithia

by Katherine Paterson

Jeannette Sanderson

0-439-29816-4

10 9 8 7 6 5 4 3 2 04 05 06 07 08

Composition by Brad Walrod/High Text Graphics, Inc.
Cover and interior design by Red Herring Design

Printed in the U.S.A. 23
First printing, June 2004

Contents

About Katherine Paterson

"I write as a way to struggle with the questions life throws at me. I write for the young because we seem to be wrestling with the same questions."

—Katherine Paterson (1999)

Katherine Paterson, one of the most admired and honored children's-book authors today, did not grow up thinking she would one day be a writer. "I loved books," she has said, "and I read a great deal, but I never imagined that I might write them."

Katherine Paterson was born on October 31, 1932, in Huayin (formerly Qing Jiang), China. Her parents, George and Mary Womeldorf, were in China working as missionaries, doing religious and charitable work, on behalf of the Presbyterian Church.

Words were important to Paterson from the beginning. "My mother read to us regularly," she has said, "and because it opened up such a wonderful world, I taught myself to read before I entered school. Soon afterwards I began to write."

When war broke out between China and Japan in 1937, Katherine and her family were forced to leave China. They relocated to North Carolina. Between the ages of five and eighteen, she moved eighteen times and attended thirteen different schools. "I remember the many schools I attended in those years mostly as places where I felt fear and humiliation. I was small, poor, and foreign. . . . I was a misfit both in the classroom and on the playground," Paterson has said.

The author remembers that when she was in first grade she came home from school on February 14 without a single valentine. Years later, her mother asked her why she never wrote a story about the time she didn't get any valentines. Paterson recalls responding, "But, Mother, *all* my stories are about the time I didn't get any valentines." Memories of being left out are woven throughout Paterson's writing.

When Katherine was in fifth grade she earned her classmates' respect by writing plays for them to act out. She still didn't want to be a writer, however. "When I was ten," Paterson has said, "I wanted to be either a movie star or a missionary."

Katherine graduated from high school in 1950 and went on to earn a bachelor's degree in English literature from King College in Bristol, Tennessee, in 1954. She then taught sixth grade for one year in rural Lovettsville, Virginia (the future setting of *Bridge to Terabithia*), before going on to earn a master's degree in Christian education.

During graduate school, a teacher suggested to Paterson that she ought to become a writer. "I was appalled," she remembers. "'I don't want to add another mediocre writer to the world,' I said."

The teacher told her that if she wasn't willing to risk mediocrity, she would never accomplish anything. But Katherine didn't pursue writing. Instead, following in her parents' footsteps, she became a missionary. A friend suggested she go to Japan, and Paterson ended up falling in love with the people and the country. In fact, she set her first children's novels in Japan.

In 1961 she went back to school at Union Theological Seminary in New York City for further study in Christian education. There Katherine met and fell in love with a fellow student, John Paterson, a Presbyterian minister. The couple married in 1962, and Katherine Paterson received her second master's degree in religious education that same year.

Paterson taught at the Pennington School for Boys in Pennington, New Jersey, until her first son was born in 1964. The Paterson family grew quickly: Within several years, the Patersons had one more son and adopted two daughters.

The year of her first child's birth was also the year Paterson accepted her first professional assignment as a writer. She was asked to create Sunday school curriculum units for the Presbyterian Church. Paterson has said, "I became a writer... without ever formulating the ambition to become one. When the curriculum assignment was completed, I turned to fiction, because that is what I most enjoy reading."

Paterson didn't become an overnight success. "I didn't know that wanting to write fiction and being able to write fiction were two quite separate things," she has said. "In the cracks of time between feedings, diapering, cooking, reading aloud, walking to the park, . . . I wrote and wrote, and published practically nothing." Paterson does not feel the time was wasted. "All those years when I couldn't sell my stories," she has said, "I was learning how to write."

Paterson's persistence proved that practice makes perfect, or pretty close. In 1973 she published her first novel, *The Sign of the Chrysanthemum.* In 1977 her third book, *The Master Puppeteer,* won the National Book Award in Children's Literature.

Paterson's fourth and most popular book, *Bridge to Terabithia,* was published in 1977 and won the 1978 John Newbery Medal.

Since then, Paterson has written more than thirty books. She has twice won both the National Book Award and the American Library Association's John Newbery Medal. And in 1998 the International Board on Books for Young People awarded Paterson the Hans Christian Andersen Medal—considered the world's most prestigious award in children's literature.

Paterson lives in Barre, Vermont, with her husband of more than forty years. What does she do in her free time? "I love to read," Paterson has said. "I love to sing. I play both the piano and tennis badly, but still like to do them. I have a wonderful family."

And, happily, she continues to write. "My gift seems to be that I am one of those fortunate people who can, if she works hard at it, uncover a story that children will enjoy."

How *Bridge to Terabithia* Came About

"Our son David's best friend...was struck and killed by lightning. It was trying to make sense of that tragedy that inspired me to write the book."

—Katherine Paterson

The year 1974 was a difficult one for the Paterson family. In the spring, Katherine Paterson was diagnosed with cancer. She had a successful operation to remove the tumor, but the experience frightened her and her family. They hadn't yet recovered from this brush with death when eight-year-old David Paterson's best friend, Lisa Hill, was struck and killed by lightning. "The two events were almost more than we could bear," Paterson has said.

So when she went to a meeting of children's-book writers and publishers in Washington, D.C., and someone asked her how her children were, she didn't answer with her usual "Fine." Instead, she poured out the tragic tale of Lisa Hill's death and her son David's grief. When she finished the story, a book editor said, "I know this sounds just like an editor, but you ought to write that story."

Not sure what else to do, Paterson began writing. "I wrote *Bridge to Terabithia* because I couldn't do anything else," she has said. "Of course, if I could've done anything I *wanted* to do, I would've brought Lisa back from the dead. But I couldn't do that, and I couldn't even comfort my son, who was totally distraught. So I did what writers often do when they can't do what they really want to do. They write a story to make sense of something that doesn't make sense. . . . So that's why I began to write the book. And people always want me to say that it comforted my son, but no, it was really for me."

Paterson wrote quickly at first, dozens and dozens of pages. But then one day, she says, she found herself "totally frozen. The time had come for my fictional child to die, and I could not let it happen."

Paterson put the book aside until a friend asked how it was coming along. "I can't let her die," Paterson told her friend. "I can't face going through Lisa's death again."

"Katherine," her friend said, "I don't think it's Lisa's death you can't face, it's yours."

Hearing those words gave Paterson the push she needed to finish the book. "If it was my death I could not face," she said, "then by God, I would face it." Within a few weeks, Paterson had finished the first draft of the book.

"I discovered gradually and not without a little pain that you don't put together a bridge for a child. You become one—you lay yourself across the chasm," Paterson has said. "In writing this book, I have thrown my body across the chasm that most terrified me."

Paterson hopes *Bridge to Terabithia* will help children deal with death by giving them practice before it actually happens. "I feel that *Bridge* is kind of a rehearsal that you go through to mourn somebody's death that you care about," Paterson has said.

While *Bridge to Terabithia* got its start in fact, Paterson has told her readers it is entirely fiction. "*Bridge* is loosely based on my son's friendship and the death of his friend. But the resemblance stops there because they [David and Jess, Lisa and Leslie] are very different people. Their families are different. They live in a different place. So it is fiction and not fact, but it grew out of a real incident."

An Interview with Katherine Paterson

About *Bridge to Terabithia*

◆ *You wrote* Bridge to Terabithia *after your eight-year-old son's best friend, Lisa Hill, was struck and killed by lightning. How did writing this book help you? How do you think this book might help others?*

Lisa's death made no sense to me. It was tragic, totally unexpected, devastating. I did what writers often do when they can't make sense out of life. I tried to shape my question into a story. Stories have to make sense—not in a logical, reasonable sense so much as an emotional sense. The ending has to somehow clarify for the reader (and first, the writer) the beginning and middle.

◆ *Terabithia was Jess and Leslie's secret place. You've said that you had lots of Terabithias as a child, and that now your secret place is inside of you. Why do you think people need secret places?*

My feeling is that if you don't have a secret place—a place where your imagination can run wild and you can ask yourself any question with no one censoring your thoughts—it's hard to grow either spiritually or intellectually. You may just keep trying to be and think what those around you seem to want.

◆ Bridge to Terabithia *has been criticized by some for its profanity and disrespect for adults, and was on People for the American Way's list of challenged books four times in the 1990s. What do you say to the people who want to remove this book from classrooms and libraries?*

Well, first, I'd hope they would read the whole book for themselves with as open a mind as possible. Then I would ask that they leave the book for the many people who have read it and found profound comfort in it. I don't think they would have been able to find that comfort if Jesse Aarons had not seemed real to them. He speaks like children I have known in that part of the world. I tried to be true to the child he was, not make him an example of proper language or behavior.

◆ *You used the Japanese word* banzai, *which means "hooray!" and "live forever," in the dedication of* Bridge to Terabithia. *Why did you choose this word?*

Because when I thought of the friendships between David and Lisa and Jess and Leslie that is how I felt.

About being a writer

◆ *When do you write? Will you describe a typical day for us?*

I am a morning person. Often during the first draft of the book I'll get up at about 5:30 A.M. to write. Nobody else much is awake. No one calls me on the phone or rings the doorbell. Nor is my critical, judgmental mind awake yet. I can play with a book like a child plays, and no one is there to interrupt or criticize. When I am rewriting, which is where the real fun comes, it doesn't matter who calls or criticizes, I'm having too much fun to let it bother me much.

◆ *You have said that the hardest part of writing a book is getting started, yet you've managed to start, and finish, about thirty books. How do you get over this difficult hurdle?*

Oh, dear. If I could answer that one, I'd have a lot more than thirty books to my credit. I spend a lot of time just fiddling around with ideas, throwing most of them away, until finally one magic day, the cluster of ideas that will become a book comes together and I can begin.

◆ *Lots of writers—young and old—hate revisions, yet you love them. Why? Also, about how many times do you revise each book before it is done?*

As I have often said: Revisions are about the only place in life where spilt milk can be turned into ice cream. I love revisions because you can take that big chunk of granite you blasted out of the earth and hoisted out (the first draft) and use your fine chisels and tools and turn it into something beautiful. Each book is different. I just keep writing until three people love it: 1. me 2. my husband 3. my editor.

◆ *What's your favorite thing about being a writer? What is your least favorite?*

I love, I am overwhelmed by, the mysterious, almost mystical relationship between writer and reader. I am thrilled whenever something that came out of my depths touches someone else in a deep way.

I guess the hardest thing—therefore what I must like least—is getting started. I find ideas worthy of a book very hard to come by.

◆ *What advice do you have for children who would like to be writers? What do you suggest they write about?*

Read. Read. Read. That's the way you learn how language works, how stories, essays, and poetry work. Write, too, of course, but not instead of reading.

When I first started trying to be a writer (and I was more than thirty years old) people kept saying, "Write what you know." Well, if I wrote what I knew, I could hardly write. I write to find out, mostly. I think you should write what you are most passionate about or what you most want to know about or explore. Don't write about anything unless you care deeply about it.

General

- *You moved eighteen times by the time you were eighteen. How has having moved around so much as a child influenced the stories you tell, the books you write?*

  I was constantly the outsider looking in. I think most writers are.

- *You have said that discovering the school library when you were a child saved your life. How do books have the power to save and to heal?*

  The library gave me books where I found friends—other children like myself who were lonely and frightened and friendless. Also, unlike the playground, where I was bullied, and the classroom where I was humiliated, the library was a safe, accepting environment. I do love librarians.

- *Which of the books you read as a child would you recommend to a ten- to twelve-year-old reader today?*

  The Yearling was my favorite book when I was eleven–twelve. I still love it.

◆ *You describe yourself as a very private person who is also a show-off. How does writing satisfy these contrary aspects of your personality?*

When I took a personality test a number of years ago, I fell off the introverted side of the chart. This doesn't mean I don't like people. I do. It just means that being with people, especially when I'm playing famous person, is exhausting to me. I come home a zombie. But closed up in my little study writing for a day fills me with life and energy. It may seem contradictory to say that I love to perform. I acted in many plays when I was young and adored it. But performing is quite different from trying to have a conversation with someone you've just met. I keep practicing, though. I want to be friendly in these situations, but it's hard for me.

◆ *What's one thing, besides writing, that you're really good at? What's one thing that you're really bad at?*

I'm good at reading, especially out loud. Sports, alas. I love sports and went out for sports in school, practiced every afternoon and sat on the bench every game. I don't like to watch sports much. I want to be part of the team. I guess that's why I like singing in the choir. I'm part of a team and haven't been benched yet.

Chapter Charter: Questions to Guide Your Reading

The following questions will help you think about the important parts of each chapter.

Chapter 1

- Why does Jess want to be the fastest kid at Lark Creek Elementary School?
- How important do you think it is to be the best at something?
- What is Jess's family like? How is it like your family? How is it unlike your family?

Chapter 2

- Why doesn't Jess show his drawings to his dad? How do you think it must feel to have to hide something you love from someone you love?
- Why is Miss Edmunds the only person Jess shows his drawings to? How important do you think it is for Jess to have someone like Miss Edmunds in his life?
- How does Jess's family add to his feelings of loneliness?
- Why doesn't Jess seem very interested in befriending Leslie when they first meet?

Chapter 3

- Does Leslie worry much about what people think of her? What about Jess? Which of these two characters are you more like?

- Why does Jess try to keep his distance from Leslie?
- Do you think Jess should have spoken up and asked Leslie if she wanted to run? Why or why not? Do you think you would have?
- What does Leslie mean when she says to Jess, "You're the only kid in this whole durned school who's worth shooting"?

Chapter 4

- Why do you think Miss Edmunds chooses to sing "Free to Be . . . You and Me" after meeting Leslie?
- What makes Jess change his mind about Leslie? How does he feel about the way he'd acted before?
- Why do Leslie's classmates make fun of her when they find out she doesn't have a television set? Why do some people have a hard time accepting other people's differences?
- What are some ways Jess shows he's brave, even when he's scared?
- Jess's mother implies that his father likes Jess playing with Leslie about as much as he likes his son drawing. And although Jess hides his drawings from his father, he does not hide Leslie. Why?
- Why does Jess write about football when Mrs. Myers asks the class to write about their favorite hobbies? What is really Jess's favorite hobby? What does Leslie write about? What would you write about?
- What are some of the major differences between Jess's and Leslie's families?
- What do you think Leslie and Jess bring to each other in their friendship?

Chapter 5

- Do you think Jess and Leslie are right or wrong to write a letter to Janice Avery and pretend it is from Willard Hughes? What would you have done, if anything, to get back at Janice for the trouble she caused you and others?
- How does Jess feel about leaving the letter for Janice? How does Leslie feel?

Chapter 6

- Why is it so important to Jess that he give Leslie something special for Christmas?
- Why is Christmas such an unhappy holiday at Jess's house? What does Jess do to try to make it happier?

Chapter 7

- Why is Jess jealous of Leslie's father?
- How does helping to fix up Leslie's house help Jess feel better about himself?
- What do you think of the "rule" at Lark Creek that "you never mixed up troubles at home with life at school"? Do you think the two can be kept separate? Do you think they should be kept separate?
- Why do you think it's so important to Jess and Leslie that Terabithia be kept secret?

Chapter 8

- How might Jess's father being laid off affect Jess and the rest of his family?
- Why do you think Jess's mother worries that Leslie pokes her nose up at her family?

- What is May Belle worried will happen if Leslie dies? Why isn't Leslie worried? Do you think she should be?

Chapter 9

- Why does Jess continue to go to Terabithia even though he becomes increasingly afraid of swinging across the rain-swollen creek?
- Do you think Jess should be ashamed of being afraid to go to Terabithia? Why or why not?
- Have you ever been as afraid of something as Jess is of the water? If so, how did you handle your fear?

Chapter 10

- What do you think Leslie would have said or done if Jess told her that he didn't want to go to Terabithia because he was afraid of swinging over the creek?
- Do you think it's wrong for Jess to be glad to be alone with Miss Edmunds? Do you think he should have thought of asking if Leslie could come with them when she had called? Why or why not?
- How do you think Jess will feel when he learns that Leslie died while he was out enjoying a perfect day with Miss Edmunds?

Chapter 11

- Why is it so hard for Jess to believe that Leslie is dead?
- Have you ever tried to pretend something bad didn't happen, the way Jess does?

Chapter 12

- Why does Jess throw the paints and paper Leslie gave him into the stream?
- Why does Jess say he hates Leslie when he doesn't mean it?
- How do Jess's father's words comfort Jess?
- What do you think of the way Jess treats May Belle, especially when he hits her in the face? Do you think he should try to make it up to her? If so, how?

Chapter 13

- Jess wonders if Terabithia is still Terabithia after Leslie's death. What do you think?
- How do you think Leslie would have felt about the funeral wreath Jess makes for her?
- How does Jess finally come to accept that it's OK to be scared sometimes?
- How does Mrs. Myers surprise Jess after Leslie's death? Did she surprise you?
- Do you agree with Jess that "it was up to him to pay back to the world in beauty and caring what Leslie had loaned him in vision and strength"? How does Jess begin to do this at the end of the book?

Plot: What's Happening?

"'We need a place,' she said, 'just for us. It would be so secret that we would never tell anyone in the whole world about it. . . . It might be a whole secret country . . . and you and I would be the rulers of it.'"

—Leslie, *Bridge to Terabithia*

Bridge to Terabithia is a story of true friendship and tragic loss. Ten-year-olds Jesse Aarons and Leslie Burke live in a world that often doesn't understand them. When Leslie moves to Jess's town, the two become best friends and create a magical place where they help each other grow strong. Jess must later call on his newfound strength to help him cope with Leslie's tragic death.

The book begins as summer is winding down. Jess awakens early to go out and run in the cow field. Jess has been working hard to make sure that he will be the fastest runner in the fifth grade.

For one day last year, Jess had been "the fastest kid in the third, fourth, *and* fifth grades" at Lark Creek Elementary. Jess enjoyed beating everyone in the race because it made people look at him differently. Up until that day, he'd been "that crazy little kid that draws all the time." Jess loves to draw, but almost no one in his family or community respects his ability. Being the fastest runner is a way for Jess to earn everyone's respect.

The next morning, Jess meets Leslie Burke. She tells him, "I thought we might as well be friends. There's no one else close by."

The next time Jess sees Leslie close-up is the first day of school. Like him, she is in Mrs. Myers's fifth-grade class. Leslie is wearing faded cutoffs, a blue undershirt, and sneakers, but no socks. Everyone else is dressed in his or her Sunday best.

During recess, the boys gather to race. Jess is surprised when Leslie Burke comes up beside him and asks him if he's running. "Later," he says, refusing to look at her, hoping "she would go back to the upper field where she belonged." But Leslie stays and Jess asks Leslie if she wants to run. "Sure," she says, grinning. "Why not?" He tells her she can run in the fourth heat with him.

As Jess watches the first three heats, he is more and more confident that he will be the fastest kid in fifth grade. Then it is time for the fourth heat. Jess is running hard when he feels, then sees, someone moving up beside him, then pulling ahead. "The faded cutoffs crossed the line a full three feet ahead of him."

The only consolation to this disappointing start of school is Miss Edmunds's visit to Lark Creek Elementary on Friday. Jess watches as the music teacher greets Leslie with a smile and begins singing "Free to Be . . . You and Me." Jess turns to Leslie and smiles at her. Leslie smiles back. And Jess "felt there in the teachers' room that it was the beginning of a new season in his life."

One day after school, Jess and Leslie are taking turns swinging on a rope across a dry creek bed when Leslie has an idea. "We need a place," she says, "just for us. It would be so secret that we would never tell anyone in the whole world about it." She goes on to say that it might be a whole secret country and that she and Jess would be its rulers.

And so they create Terabithia, a magic kingdom in the woods that can be reached only by swinging across the creek bed on the enchanted rope. Jess and Leslie both think it is perfect. "In the shadowy light of the stronghold everything seemed possible."

Jess and Leslie are soon spending nearly all their free time together. Jess's older sisters and his classmates tease him about hanging around with a girl. His parents worry about their only son playing with only girls. But Jess doesn't care what these people say. "For the first time in his life he got up every morning with something to look forward to. Leslie was more than his friend. She was his other, more exciting self—his way to Terabithia and all the worlds beyond."

As winter turns to spring, Jess and Leslie continue going to Terabithia, but Jess does so with increasing unease. All March it poured, and for the first time in many years there is water in the creek bed, "enough so that when they swung across, it was a little scary looking down at the rushing water below."

It is raining on Easter Monday, but Jess and Leslie go to Terabithia anyway. When they see how high the stream is, Jess suggests that they forget about going over. But Leslie wants to go. "C'mon, Jess. We can make it," she says. And they do.

The next morning Jess wakes filled with anxiety about the creek and about telling Leslie that he doesn't want to cross it. "It wasn't so much that he minded telling Leslie that he was afraid to go; it was that he minded being afraid." Then, Miss Edmunds calls and asks him to go to Washington with her, to visit the Smithsonian or the National Gallery. Jess is thrilled. After they are on their way, Jess thinks that he might have asked Miss Edmunds if Leslie could have come.

When Jess gets home from his perfect day with Miss Edmunds, his mother sobs and cries out, "O my God. O my God," when she sees him.

"Your girl friend's dead," Brenda says, "and Momma thought you was dead, too."

His father explains that they found Leslie in the creek that morning. "That old rope you kids been swinging on broke," he says. "They think she musta hit her head on something when she fell."

At first, Jess refuses to believe him. When he does accept the truth, however, he is very angry at Leslie for leaving him.

The next day, Jess uses a large branch to cross over to Terabithia. He wants to do something to mourn Leslie's death.

He makes a funeral wreath and solemnly carries it to the sacred grove. "Father," he says, "into Thy hands I commend her spirit."

Then Jess hears his sister May Belle crying for help. She tried to follow him to Terabithia, but froze in fear halfway across the tree branch Jess had put across the creek. Jess slowly helps her across. When May Belle tells Jess how she got scared, Jess tells her that's okay. "Everybody gets scared sometimes," he says. "You don't have to be ashamed."

Jess comes to believe "that perhaps Terabithia was like a castle where you came to be knighted. After you stayed for a while and grew strong, you had to move on." He decides it is time for him to move on. "It was up to him to pay back to the world in beauty and caring what Leslie had loaned him in vision and strength."

Jess begins doing this by building a bridge to Terabithia. When he is finished, he puts flowers in May Belle's hair and leads her across the bridge, telling her that all the Terabithians are standing on tiptoe to see her. "There's a rumor going around that the beautiful girl arriving today might be the queen they've been waiting for," Jess tells her.

Thinking about the plot

- Why is Jess reluctant to be friends with Leslie in the beginning of the story?
- What do Jess and Leslie give to each other in their friendship?
- Why is Terabithia so important to Jess and Leslie?

Setting/Time and Place: Where in the World Are We?

"In the shadowy light of the stronghold everything seemed possible."

—*Bridge to Terabithia*

Time: When does the story take place?

Bridge to Terabithia is a contemporary novel, meaning it was written about the current time period. Since it was published more than twenty-five years ago, however, it is not contemporary to today's readers.

We can see that the story is set in the mid-1970s in a number of ways. One of these is through a comment about the "recent" Vietnam War, which actually ended in 1975. Also, during the 1960s and 1970s there was a great deal of protest against the United States' involvement in that war. People who supported the war sometimes called those who opposed it "peaceniks." This is a name that some of the children in the book call Miss Edmunds.

"Hippie," another name Jess's mom and some of the children call Miss Edmunds, also places the book in the 1970s. "Hippie" is a word that was commonly used at that time to describe a person who did not dress and act as most people did, and Miss

Edmunds definitely stood out from the rest of Jess's community. Jess notes that the kids "make fun of Miss Edmunds's lack of lipstick or the cut of her jeans," which made her different from the other women—female teachers or parents—they knew.

Comments about fashion help show when the story takes place. We learn that Miss Edmunds was the only female teacher at Lark Creek Elementary who wore pants. Today it is common for women to wear pants, but at the time the book was written, it was still unusual, especially outside of big cities.

Place: Where are we?

The book is set in a fictional rural Virginia town. Paterson created the town, which she calls Lark Creek, based on her memories of living and teaching sixth grade for one year in rural Lovettsville, Virginia. "I have to know about a place before I write a story that is set in that place," Paterson has said.

What is Lark Creek like? It is a rural, poor, and, in many ways, a narrow-minded place. It is also a place containing great physical beauty, for those willing to see it.

Paterson establishes the rural setting in a number of ways. She begins the book with Jess running in his family's cow field. Milking the cow is one of Jess's chores. Another is picking beans from the bean patch and helping his mother can them. These are all activities that take place in a rural setting.

The author tells us more about the rural setting when she describes Jess's father's long ride back and forth to Washington, D.C., where he works digging and hauling all day. Mr. Aarons's ride is so long because the family lives in the country, many, many miles from the city.

While rural places are not always poor, that is sometimes the case. As Jess tells Leslie, "You can't make a go of a farm nowadays, you know. My dad has to go to Washington to work, or we wouldn't have enough money. . . ." When Leslie tells him that money is not a problem for her family, Jess is surprised. "He did not know people for whom money was not the problem."

It is clear that money *is* a problem for Jess's family. His house is so small that Jess shares a bedroom with his two younger sisters. Jess's worn sneakers, his one pair of corduroy pants, and his lack of boots show the reader how tight money is. When Jess draws, he uses whatever paper and pencils he can get hold of. But he dreams of more. "Lord, what he wouldn't give for a new pad or real art paper and a set of those marking pens."

As Christmas approaches, the stress of not having enough money puts a strain on the entire family. Jess worries about what he can give Leslie: "His dad had told him he would give him a dollar for each member of the family, but even if he cheated on the family presents, there was no way he could get from that enough to buy Leslie anything worth giving her."

Most people in Lark Creek are as poor as the Aaronses. The lack of money in the town is evident at Jess's school. Lark Creek

Elementary is so crowded that Jess's class of thirty-one students is jammed into a small basement room, music is held in the teachers' room, and there is no gym. In addition, the school is short on supplies, "especially athletic equipment, so all the balls went to the upper grades at recess time after lunch." That's why Jess and the other lower-grade boys take up running during recess: It's a sport that doesn't require any special equipment.

Paterson shows us Lark Creek's prejudices when she tells us how angry Jess's father was when Jess told him he wanted to be an artist when he grew up. "Bunch of old ladies turning my only son into some kind of a—," he said. And even though he stopped on the word, "Jess had gotten the message. It was one you didn't forget."

Jess's family and schoolmates are just as narrow-minded about his friendship with Leslie as they are about his love of drawing. His older sisters call Leslie Jess's "*girl* friend" and his mother says that she is sure Jess's father is "fretting that his only son did nothing but play with girls, and they both were worried about what would come of it."

Jess and Leslie cope with the narrowness of the world around them by creating their own imaginary kingdom, where they are king and queen. They build Terabithia's stronghold in the woods beyond the creek behind Leslie's house. While the woods are there for all to enjoy, only Jess and Leslie seem to appreciate their beauty and magic. "As a regular thing, as a permanent place, this was where he would choose to be," Jess thinks of the spot where they build their stronghold. "Here where the dogwood and redbud played hide and seek between the oaks and evergreens, and the sun flung itself in golden streams through the trees to splash warmly at their feet."

Thinking about the setting

- What are some of the clues that *Bridge to Terabithia* takes place in a rural community?
- How is Lark Creek like where you live? How is it different?
- Do you think *Bridge to Terabithia* would change much if it were rewritten so that it took place in the early twenty-first century rather than the late twentieth century? Why or why not?

Themes/Layers of Meaning: Is That What It *Really* Means?

"For the first time in his life, he got up every morning with something to look forward to. Leslie was more than his friend. She was his other, more exciting self—his way to Terabithia and all the worlds beyond."

—*Bridge to Terabithia*

Friendship

The value of friendship is one of the major themes in *Bridge to Terabithia.* It is through friendship that Jess and Leslie are able to accept themselves, feel a sense of belonging, and grow.

Before Jess meets Leslie, he feels all alone in the world. His father works long hours and is too tired to pay much attention to him when he is home. He has his mother and four sisters, but "sometimes he felt so lonely among all those females." At school, Jess has no real friends, except for Miss Edmunds, the music teacher. So when Leslie moves in, Jess is ripe for friendship.

But initially Jess is not interested in being Leslie's friend. First off, she's a girl. And not only that, she's a girl who "had no notion of what you did and didn't do," as she proves when she joins the boys for races at recess.

Jess doesn't appreciate Leslie for being herself, despite the fact that he is so often torn between being himself—a sensitive boy who loves to draw—and being what others expect him to be. It isn't until music class that first week of school that Jess reveals his real self and smiles at Leslie in a way that tells her he wants to be friends.

Leslie enriches Jess's life in ways he could never have imagined. She encourages him to use his imagination in ways that go far beyond drawing. She tells Jess stories and lends him books. She believes in him. When Leslie tells Jess, "You should draw a picture of Terabithia for us to hang in the castle," Jess responds, "I can't. . . . I just can't get the poetry of the trees." Leslie reassures him, "Don't worry. You will someday."

In return, Jess gives Leslie the comfort of his friendship, which helps her survive in a world that is far different from the one she left behind. Jess also teaches Leslie about caring for others. When she finds Janice Avery crying in the girls' room and doesn't want to do anything to help her, Jess says, "You're the one who's always telling me I gotta care."

Accepting differences

Bridge to Terabithia is also about being different and accepting your differences as well as those of others.

Jess is different from the people around him. He likes to draw and wants to be an artist when he grows up. But many in Jess's community do not respect art; even his father thinks being an artist is not very manly.

In the beginning of the story, Jess tries to hide his differences. In one instance, when Mrs. Myers asks the class to write a paper about their favorite hobby, "Jess had written about football, which he really hated, but he had enough brains to know that if he said drawing, everyone would laugh at him."

But then Jess meets Leslie, who is also different, but is accepting of her differences as well as those of others. Leslie shows her comfort with who she is when she joins the boys for races during recess. Leslie loves to run and doesn't care if only boys have run in the past.

At first, Jess is annoyed by the way Leslie marches to the beat of her own drummer. "Lord," he thinks, "the girl had no notion of what you did and didn't do." It is Miss Edmunds, Jess's "fellow outlaw," who helps Jess accept Leslie, and they both help Jess accept himself. When Miss Edmunds sings "Free to Be. . .You and Me" after meeting Leslie, Jess finds himself smiling at Leslie.

Later, when the two are best friends, Jess must listen to the taunts of his sisters and his schoolmates about having a "*girl* friend." Even his mother and father disapprove of him spending so much time with a girl. But Jess doesn't care. He is learning to accept who he is.

Imagination

The importance of imagination is another theme Paterson weaves into *Bridge to Terabithia.* Without imagination, life can be pretty dreary, which is how Jess's life is before he meets Leslie. Until she arrives in Lark Creek, Jess's only imaginative outlet is drawing. But when Leslie arrives, she uses her imagination, and encourages Jess to use his, to create a magical new world where the two of them can be themselves and so much more.

"He grabbed the end of the rope and swung out toward the other bank with a kind of wild exhilaration and landed gently on his feet, taller and stronger and wiser in that mysterious land." This imaginative kingdom is not only a place where Jess and Leslie are taller and stronger, it is also a place where fears are forgotten: "Between the two of them they owned the world and no enemy . . . could ever really defeat them."

When Leslie dies, Jess wonders if the magic is lost, but discovers that it isn't—it is still inside him. And it is inside May Belle, too, though she may not be aware of it until Jess shows it to her: "He put flowers in her hair and led her across the bridge—the great bridge into Terabithia—which might look to someone with no magic in him like a few planks across a nearly dry gully."

Fear

Fear and learning to accept one's fears is another important theme in *Bridge to Terabithia.* Before he becomes more self-accepting, Jess is ashamed of his fears. He is afraid to befriend

Leslie, and when he finally does, he is angry at himself for having waited. “He smiled at her. What the heck? There wasn’t any reason he couldn’t. What was he scared of anyhow? Lord. Sometimes he acted like the original yellow-bellied sapsucker.”

When Jess listens to Leslie’s scuba diving essay, “he could hardly breathe,” because he can’t swim and is afraid of the water. Again, he is ashamed. “Lord, he was such a coward. . . . He was worse a baby than Joyce Ann.”

And when the creek bed fills with water, Jess becomes afraid to cross it to get to Terabithia. “For Jess the fear of the crossing rose with the height of the creek.” He doesn’t know what to do. “It wasn’t so much that he minded telling Leslie that he was afraid to go; it was that he minded being afraid.”

Jess refuses to let fear get the better of him, though. He decides he’ll ask Leslie to teach him to swim come summer. “I’ll just grab that old terror by the shoulders and shake the daylights out of it.”

But Leslie dies before he can ask her. And Jess wonders if she was scared. *“Did you know you were dying?”* he wonders. *“Were you scared like me?”*

When May Belle tries to follow him over to Terabithia and nearly falls in the creek, Jess rescues her. When May Belle tells him she was scared, he tells her it’s okay. “Everybody gets scared sometimes, May Belle. You don’t have to be ashamed.”

And as Jess looks to the future, he seems to be more at ease with his fears. "As for the terrors ahead—for he did not fool himself that they were all behind him—well, you just have to stand up to your fear and not let it squeeze you white."

Caring for others

Another theme in *Bridge to Terabithia* relates to the importance of caring for others. We see it especially when Leslie finds Janice Avery crying in the bathroom, and Jess wants to do something to help her. "Lord, what was the matter with him? Janice Avery had given him nothing but trouble, and now he was feeling responsible for her." Despite Leslie's initial reluctance, Jess talks her into going back into the girls' room to try to help Janice.

Miss Edmunds also shows the importance of caring for others. She does this by paying special attention to Jess, encouraging him in his artwork, and taking him to the National Gallery and the Smithsonian.

May Belle shows how much she cares when she tries to follow Jess to Terabithia, even after he hit her in the face. "I just wanted to find you," she tells him, "so you wouldn't be so lonesome."

Giving

The value of giving and giving back is another theme that runs through this book. One of the first and most natural places we see this giving is at Christmastime. Jess wants to give Leslie the perfect gift. "It was not that she would expect something expensive; it was that he needed to give her something as much as he needed to eat when he was hungry."

Jess does find the perfect gift for Leslie—a puppy. And she gives him a wonderful gift of paper, brushes, and paint in return.

We also see the value of giving when Jess goes over his budget to give May Belle the Barbie that she wants for Christmas. Later, when Jess thinks about doing something nice for Mrs. Myers, he tells the reader, "Sometimes like the Barbie doll you need to give people something that's for them, not just something that makes you feel good giving it."

When Jess realizes all that Leslie has given him, he feels that he must find a way to reciprocate. "It was up to him to pay back to the world in beauty and caring what Leslie had loaned him in vision and strength." One way he does this is by building a bridge and leading May Belle into Terabithia.

Death

Another important theme in *Bridge to Terabithia* is death. Jess must learn to accept his best friend's death, despite feeling that "Leslie could not die any more than he himself could die."

Jess reacts to the news of Leslie's death with shock, selfishness, anger, and grief. At first, Jess does not believe his father when he tells him that Leslie has died: "No! I don't believe you. You're lying to me!"

When Jess goes to see Leslie's parents, he finds himself filled with conflicted emotions. He feels briefly elated to think "he was the only person his age he knew whose best friend had died. It made him important." He feels annoyed at all the adults crying around him: "They weren't crying for Leslie. They were crying for themselves." And he feels angry, angry that Leslie's parents brought her here in the first place.

Jess is also angry at Leslie. "She had tricked him. She had made him leave his old self behind and come into her world, and then . . . she had left him stranded there." He flings the paper and paints she had given him for Christmas into the creek, crying out, "I hate her. I hate her. I wish I'd never seen her in my whole life." When his father pulls Jess onto his lap and tells him, "Hell, ain't it," Jess finds it "strangely comforting."

Thinking about the themes

- What do you think is the most important theme in *Bridge to Terabithia*?
- What did Jess and Leslie give to each other in their friendship? What do you have to offer as a friend?
- Why is it important to accept our own differences and those of others?
- How do you feel about your fears? Do you think they are something to be ashamed of? Or do you agree with Jess that "everybody gets scared sometimes. . . . You don't have to be ashamed"?

Characters: Who Are These People, Anyway?

Here is a list of the characters in *Bridge to Terabithia.* Following that, there is a brief description of each of the main characters.

Jesse Aarons	a fifth-grade boy
Leslie Burke	the new fifth-grade girl
Daddy/Mr. Aarons	Jess's father
Momma/Mrs. Aarons	Jess's mother
May Belle	Jess's six-year-old sister
Ellie, Brenda, and Joyce Ann	Jess's other sisters
Miss Edmunds	the music teacher
Mrs. Myers	the fifth-grade teacher
Janice Avery	a seventh-grade bully
Prince Terrien	the puppy Jess gives Leslie
Bill Burke	Leslie's father
Judy Burke	Leslie's mother

Jesse Aarons: Jesse, also called Jess, the main character in the book, is a ten-year-old boy who feels lost and lonely in a family and community that, for the most part, does not understand him. Jess is artistic, sensitive, fearful, kind, and hardworking.

It is clear from the beginning that Jess wants desperately to belong. He has gotten up every morning all summer to run so that when he goes back to school he can be the fastest kid in the fifth grade. Being the fastest will win him the approval of his peers; they will stop thinking of Jess as "that crazy little kid that draws all the time."

Jess also wants to be fastest to win the approval and attention of his father. Jess wants and needs his father's attention. In a house full of girls—four sisters, two older and two younger, as well as his mother—Jess feels very lonely. The only family member he feels at all close to is May Belle, and she's not even seven.

What Jess loves to do more than anything else is draw. "Jess drew the way some people drink whiskey. The peace would start at the top of his muddled brain and seep down through his tired and tensed-up body."

Drawing is Jess's comfort, but it is also what sets him apart. When he was in first grade and told his father he wanted to be an artist when he grew up, his father was furious. His teachers, all but Miss Edmunds, don't like his drawing either. Because Jess doesn't draw traditional subjects—he usually draws animals in crazy predicaments—the teachers complain that he is wasting time, talent, and supplies. Even his mother looks at Jess's drawing as a waste of time when he should be doing chores. Because Jess is sensitive, these criticisms hurt. He tries to hide his love of drawing from everyone but Miss Edmunds and Leslie.

But Jess's sensitivity is not limited to his own feelings. He feels sorry for Leslie when she joins his class. "It must be embarrassing to sit in front when you find yourself dressed funny on the first day of school. And you don't know anybody."

Jess is also sensitive to the people in his family. He gets "mad at himself for cutting her [May Belle] down," when he knows she worships him. And Jess tries to make his father feel good about the racing-car set he gave Jess for Christmas.

In addition to being very sensitive, Jess is also fearful. He is afraid of being different, of deep water, of the dark pine forest, and of Janice Avery, among other things. But during the course of the book, Jess learns to stand up and face the "whole mob of foolish little fears running riot inside his gut."

Jess is also kind. He feels sorry for Janice Avery after he and Leslie send her a love letter and pretend it's from Willard Hughes. And when Leslie says she found Janice crying in the girls' room, he talks her into going back in to see what's wrong with Janice.

Finally, Jess is hardworking. Although his mother calls him lazy, he seems anything but and is often helping around the house. In fact, over the course of just one day, Jess milks Miss Bessie, picks beans and helps his mother can them, then makes himself and his little sisters peanut butter sandwiches for supper. And he does all this after having gotten up early to run.

Leslie Burke: Leslie Burke is the other main character in this book. She is friendly, self-confident, a great runner, bright, imaginative, and seemingly fearless.

Leslie is nearly ten when she moves to Lark Creek from Arlington, Virginia. Her parents are both writers, and they moved to Lark Creek because, as Leslie explains, "they decided they were too hooked on money and success, so they bought that old farm and they're going to farm it and think about what's important." Where Leslie was once surrounded by wealth and open-mindedness, she is now surrounded by poverty and narrow-mindedness.

From the moment we first meet her, we see that Leslie is friendly. She is sitting on a fence watching Jess run. She tells him, "I thought we might as well be friends. There's no one else close by." Though Jess isn't interested in being friends at first, Leslie doesn't give up.

Leslie's self-confidence is also evident from the beginning of the story. She comes to a new school dressed unlike any of the other students and, despite the fact that they all stare at her, she doesn't seem to care. She also has the confidence to join the boys at recess and race with them. When one of the boys tells her, "You can run on up to the hopscotch now," she refuses. "But I won the heat," she says. "I want to run." And run she does, winning the race.

Leslie is smart. She is such a good student that Mrs. Myers has a smile just for her, the "Leslie Burke special." Leslie is also a wonderful writer and storyteller; her scuba diving essay is so good that her words "drew Jess with her under the dark water."

Leslie's intelligence extends to her understanding of people. From the beginning, she recognizes Jess as a good person although he tries not to show it. "You're the only kid in this whole durned school who's worth shooting," she tells him. She knows what makes the school bully, Janice Avery, tick, and is the person to figure out a satisfying form of revenge after Janice steals May Belle's Twinkies.

Imagination is one of Leslie's greatest gifts. It is the spark of Leslie's imagination that helps her and Jess escape the narrow-mindedness of the people around them and create a whole new world for themselves. They are the rulers of Terabithia, and it is there that they conquer enemies real and imagined; there that they plot revenge against Janice Avery and use sticks to fight off giants.

Finally, Leslie is seemingly fearless. She is not afraid of scuba diving or Janice Avery; of swollen creek beds or dark pine forests. Leslie's fearlessness is an inspiration to Jess.

May Belle: May Belle is one of Jess's younger sisters. "She was going on seven, and she worshiped him, which was OK sometimes." May Belle is the only one of his sisters Jess can stand to be around. His two older sisters, Ellie and Brenda, are "cagey girls who managed somehow to have all the fun and leave him and their mother with all the work." His youngest sister, Joyce Ann, "cried if you looked at her cross-eyed." Jess has a soft spot for May Belle. "She was a good kid. He really liked old May Belle."

May Belle looks up to, and looks out for, Jess. She looks up to him and encourages him in his running. She thinks he can do anything, including exact revenge on Janice Avery for stealing her Twinkies. She looks out for him after Leslie dies by trying to follow him to Terabithia. "I just wanted to find you, so you wouldn't be so lonesome," she tells him.

Daddy/Mr. Aarons: Jess's father is a quiet man who works long hours in faraway Washington, D.C., and has little time or energy for his son when he gets home from work. He is an old-fashioned man who has clear ideas regarding what boys and girls, men and women, should do. When Jess tells him he wants to be an artist when he grows up, he is very unhappy, worrying that his son is not manly enough. He worries about Jess spending so much time playing with a girl. He never hugs Jess; the only thing he might say to him all day is, "Mighty late with the milking, aren't you, son?"

But while he is old-fashioned, Jess's father is not cold, as he shows when Leslie dies. He goes after Jess when he runs away, and carries him back to the truck. He also follows Jess when he runs down to the creek and throws away all the art supplies Leslie gave him. He pulls Jess onto his lap and comforts him, knowing that his son needs his help to get through such a terrible tragedy.

Momma/Mrs. Aarons: Jess's mother, like his father, has specific ideas of what people should and shouldn't do; she also has a dread of being treated with disrespect. Her narrow-mindedness is evident in her comments about Miss Edmunds ("Sounds like some kinda hippie."), Leslie ("tacky clothes," hair "shorter than a boy's"), and Leslie's parents ("hardly more than hippies"). It is also clear in the way she treats Jess's drawing as unimportant: "Jesse Oliver!" she yells at him. "Whatcha mean lying there in the middle of the floor doing nothing anyway?"

We see one example of Mrs. Aarons's fear of disrespect after Jess asks if Leslie can go to church with them. "I don't want no one poking their nose up at my family," she says.

Miss Edmunds: Miss Edmunds is the music teacher at Lark Creek Elementary School. She is young and free-spirited, and Jess is in love with her. More than her "long swishy black hair and blue, blue eyes," Jess's love is a result of Miss Edmunds's encouragement. Miss Edmunds is the only adult who has had something positive to say about his drawings.

The music teacher is a friend to all students, especially those who are different. Upon meeting Leslie, she leads the class in singing "Free to Be . . . You and Me," encouraging the students to accept themselves as well as one another. It is this song that prompts Jess to smile at Leslie, thus beginning their wonderful friendship.

Thinking about the characters

- How does Jess Aarons grow during the course of the book?
- If someone as different as Leslie Burke moved to your school, how would you treat her? Why? Would you treat her differently after having read *Bridge to Terabithia*?
- Why do you think Jess's father feels the way he does about Jess's drawing? Why do he and his wife feel uncomfortable with Jess having a girl for a best friend?

Opinion: What Have Other People Thought About *Bridge to Terabithia*?

It's a winner!

Bridge to Terabithia has won many awards, the most prestigious of which is the 1978 John Newbery Medal. This award is given annually to the author of "the most distinguished contribution to American literature for children" published the preceding year. The selection is made by fifteen librarians on the American Library Association's Newbery Committee. Look at your copy of *Bridge to Terabithia* and you may see the award, printed in gold, on the cover.

Censored!

Despite its popularity, *Bridge to Terabithia* is often on the Banned Books List of the American Library Association. Paterson has said, "There are folks who believe that children's books should teach lessons to children. I believe they should tell a story about people as truthfully and powerfully as possible. When you tell a powerful story it nearly always seems to offend somebody."

One way in which *Bridge* offends some readers is with its use of swear words. Paterson defends her use of profanity in her characters' dialogue: "Jess and his father talk like the people I knew who lived in that area," she has said. "I believe it is my responsibility to create characters who are real, not models of good behavior. If Jess and his dad are to be real, they must speak and act like real people. I have a lot of respect for my readers. I do not expect them to imitate my characters, [but] simply to care about them and understand them."

Other critics find fault with *Bridge to Terabithia*'s subject matter; they say death is an inappropriate topic for children. Paterson disagrees. "*Bridge* is not considered appropriate for children, because death is not an appropriate topic for children—which I find very sad, because two of my children lost friends by the time they were eight years old. . . . Death was not appropriate for my children, but somehow, as their parents, we had to help them face death."

Paterson has said she hopes that her book will help others face the death of loved ones. "I feel that *Bridge* is kind of a rehearsal that you go through to mourn somebody's death that you care about. It's very *normal* to be angry when someone you love dies—even angry at the person who dies."

The author has said, "I'm always a little worried when somebody gives *Bridge* to somebody because someone has died, because I always think that it's too late. They should've read it before that."

Why are Jess's parents so mean?

Some critics complain about Paterson's portrayal of Jess's parents, saying she made them too mean. Paterson has responded: "All the parents in my stories are seen from their children's point of view, and it has been my experience that children are very seldom fair in their judgments of their parents." As for Jess's mom and dad, Paterson believes they are "doing the best they can under trying circumstances."

Thinking about what others think about *Bridge to Terabithia*

- Do you think *Bridge to Terabithia* seems like an award-winning book? What other Newbery-winning books have you read? How does *Bridge to Terabithia* compare?
- Do you agree with Paterson that it's important that her characters speak and act like real people, even if that means they use profanity? Why or why not?
- Do you agree with Paterson that reading a book like *Bridge to Terabithia* can help you deal with a death in your own life? Has reading about a difficult experience ever helped you cope with a difficult experience in your life?
- Do you think Jess's parents would have seemed so mean if the story had been told from their point of view? Do you agree with Paterson that children are seldom fair in their judgment of their parents?

Glossary

allotted set aside for a particular purpose

beseech to ask someone in a very serious way; to beg

britches pants

brood sow an adult female pig that's kept for breeding

clabber sour curdled milk

commend to put in the care of someone

complacent overly satisfied with one's situation in life

conspicuous stands out; obvious

contempt total lack of respect

discern to detect; to see with the eyes

dredge to come up with; unearth

falter to act or move in an unsteady way

flank the side of an animal, between its ribs and its hips

flounce to move in a lively or bouncy way

garish too brightly colored or overly decorated

grit the ability to keep on doing something even though it is very difficult

gunnysack a large sack made of a loosely woven coarse material

hernia a rupture or abnormal body opening

hypocritical pretending to have feelings, beliefs, or qualities that one does not have

intoxicated excited or made enthusiastic

laid off dismissed from work

liable likely

moony dreamy or absentminded

mother lode the main source or supply

parapet a low wall or railing along the edge of a roof or balcony

prospectors people who explore for valuable minerals or oil

realm a kingdom

reassess to rethink the importance of something

rooting digging around

shinny to climb by pulling with the hands and legs

siege the surrounding of a place, such as a castle or city, to cut off supplies, and then waiting for those inside to surrender

sire a form of address for a king

snare a trap for catching birds or animals

snuffled breathed noisily and with difficulty

sporadically happening at irregular intervals

stronghold a fortress or a place that is well protected against attack or danger

tidings news or information

tyrants people who rule other people in a cruel or unjust way

utterly completely or totally

vain unsuccessful or futile

Katherine Paterson on Writing

Katherine Paterson believes being a writer is "the best job in the world." The author of more than thirty books has said, "I love to write. If I'm not writing for a period of time, I feel lost."

While Paterson loves being a writer, she admits it's hard work. "You can't wait for inspiration to strike," she has said. "You go to work every morning. It's day labor."

Paterson gets her ideas "from life, observation, reading, dreams. Sometimes they just seem to come out of the blue and I have no idea of the actual source."

This author's favorite subject is people. While she always knows something about her characters before she begins a book, she really gets to know them in the writing. Before writing, "I have to know where they were born, what was happening in their family before they were born," she has said. "After I finish the first draft, I know them better. When I rewrite, I see the things that they would never have said or never have done.... So with each rewriting, I get to know them better."

While Paterson gets to know her characters as she writes, she makes sure she knows as much as possible about the setting before she begins. "I'm a great believer in research," Paterson has said. "I have to know about a place before I write a story that is set in that place."

For Paterson, one of the toughest parts of her job is writing the first draft. "First drafts are usually painful," the author has said. "The first draft is always messy and horrible." But once she's written the first draft, once she can look at it and say "Not bad," Paterson gets to begin doing what she really loves: rewriting. "A good rewrite morning is bliss," the author has said. "Where else in life can spilled milk be transformed into ice cream?"

Sometimes, Paterson can't remember the bliss. "There are days when I wonder how on earth I got involved in this madness," she has said. "Why . . . did I ever think I had anything to say that was worth putting down on paper? And there are those days when I have finished a book and can't for the life of me believe I'll ever have the wit or will to write another.

"Eventually a character or characters will walk into my imagination and begin to take over my life. I'll spend the next couple of years getting to know them and telling their story. Then the joy of writing far outweighs the struggle, and I know beyond a doubt that I am the most fortunate person in the world to have been given such work to do."

For aspiring writers

When asked what advice she has for young writers, Paterson has said, "Read, because that's the way you learn how the language works. That's the way you learn about emotion, on paper. That's where you find out how stories are fastened, by reading and reading and reading. And you just absorb it. Nobody's giving you rules in working it out. You're *learning*, and you're enjoying it while you're learning—which is very important."

The author also tells prospective writers to write. And rewrite. "My first draft is usually a mess," Paterson has said. "Sometimes I become so discouraged that I want to pitch it rather than rewrite it. . . . Never become discouraged or give up because your first draft is a mess. Work hard to revise it, even if you have to do it many, many times! Good writers are hard workers!"

Paterson's own persistence is how she got to be where she is today. "All those years when I couldn't sell my stories, I was learning how to write. I found that a writer must give her heart as well as her mind to her work. I learned to love the process of revising a book, going over and over it until I was sure it was the best I could do."

The author also tells aspiring writers to use their imaginations. "The old idea was that you have to live an exciting life to write good books," Paterson has said. "I believe that you have to have a rich imaginative life. You don't have to fight dragons to write books. You just have to live deeply the life you've been given."

- **Set the place:** Paterson is a great believer in research and has to know all about a place before she sets a story there. Think of a story you'd like to write. Where does it take place? Research that setting. Take notes to help you remember details to include in your story. For example, what is the geography like? Are there any landmarks? What is the weather like? What plants and animals are found in the area? Use these details to make a believable setting.

- **Make ice cream (in other words, revise):** Paterson says revising is a way of turning spilled milk into ice cream. Take a story, poem, or essay you have written and revise it to make it the best it can be. As you revise, ask yourself: Does this make sense? Does one idea follow another? Is this the best word I can use here? Is there too much or too little information? Is there unnecessary information?

- **Play time:** Among Paterson's first writings—when she was ten or so—were plays she wrote for her classmates to act in. Try writing a play for your family, friends, or classmates to act in. If you have difficulty writing an original play, you might want to start by adapting a short story or a book into a play, then make your next play original.

- **Favorite hobby:** In *Bridge to Terabithia*, Mrs. Myers asks her fifth-grade class to write a paper about their favorite hobby. Leslie's essay about scuba diving is so good that "the power of Leslie's words drew Jess with her under the dark water." Write a few paragraphs about your favorite hobby, and try to write it so that it has the power to move your reader or listener the way Leslie's did.

- **Draw with words:** Paterson uses wonderfully descriptive language to paint pictures that place the reader in her story. One tool she uses is *similes*, figures of speech in which two unlike things are compared using the words *like* or *as*. Here are two examples: "Surprise swooshed up from the class like steam from a released radiator cap" and "the boys quivered on the edges of their seats like moths fighting to be freed of cocoons."

Try using similes in your own writing. You might start by brainstorming a list of similes for such things as surprise, excitement, sadness, nervousness, happiness, and fear.

Activities

• **Sell the book:** Imagine you've been asked to design a cover for *Bridge to Terabithia* that will make more young people pick it up and read it. What would your cover look like? What image or images would you include on the front? Make your new cover. On the back, write a review of the book that you think will make others want to read it. Don't retell the whole story just tell enough to let a potential reader know what it is about and to interest her or him in reading the whole book.

• **Visit a museum:** When Miss Edmunds takes Jess to Washington and learns that it is his first trip to an art gallery, she says, "Great. My life has been worthwhile after all." If you've never been to a museum or art gallery, ask an adult to take you. If you have been, go again. If it's not possible to visit an art gallery in person, borrow an art book from the library and visit through photographs. As you look at the different kinds of art, whether in person or through a book, ask yourself if any of them make you feel as strongly as Jess felt when he viewed the pieces of artwork in the gallery.

• **Make a diorama:** One of the pieces of art that most moves Jess at the Smithsonian is a diorama of Indians disguised in buffalo skins scaring a herd of buffalo into stampeding over a cliff to their deaths. Jess describes this art as "a three-dimensional nightmare version of some of his own drawings." Make a diorama based on this book. It could be a copy of the one Jess saw at the Smithsonian, or it could be another scene from the book, such as Jess and Leslie racing the first day of school, swinging over to Terabithia, or Jess leading May Belle over the bridge into Terabithia.

• **Winning ways:** Katherine Paterson won the 1978 John Newbery Medal for *Bridge to Terabithia.* Read one or two other Newbery-winning books, and think about what it takes to be a winner. Some recent Newbery Medal–winning books are:

Crispin: The Cross of Lead by Avi (2003)
A Single Shard by Linda Sue Park (2002)
A Year Down Yonder by Richard Peck (2001)
Bud, Not Buddy by Christopher Paul Curtis (2000)
Holes by Louis Sachar (1999)
Out of the Dust by Karen Hesse (1998)
The View from Saturday by E. L. Konigsburg (1997)
The Midwife's Apprentice by Karen Cushman (1996)
Walk Two Moons by Sharon Creech (1995)
The Giver by Lois Lowry (1994)
Missing May by Cynthia Rylant (1993)

• **Draw Terabithia:** Leslie tells Jess, "You should draw a picture of Terabithia for us to hang in the castle." Jess says, "I can't. . . . I just can't get the poetry of the trees." See if you can get the poetry of the trees. Draw a picture of Terabithia as you imagine it to be.

• **What is a hippie?:** Jess's mom and many of his classmates call Miss Edmunds a hippie. Research what a hippie is, and decide for yourself whether or not Miss Edmunds fits that description. After that, decide whether you think being a hippie is a good or bad thing and why Jess's parents and his classmates might think it's a bad thing.

- **"Free to Be...You and Me":** Find the words to the 1972 song "Free to Be...You and Me" that Miss Edmunds sings when she first meets Leslie. Then, make a picture book about the importance of being yourself by using the lyrics and your own illustrations.

- **Washington, D.C., landmarks:** When Jess is driving into Washington with Miss Edmunds, he recognizes all the landmarks, "looking surprisingly the way the books had pictured them." Imagine you are planning a trip to Washington. Research the landmarks. Then, make a simple map for yourself showing where these landmarks are in relation to one another. Be sure to include the two places Jess visited: the National Gallery and the Smithsonian.

- **Make a trail mix:** In Terabithia, Jess and Leslie snack on crackers and dried fruit. You can make your own special snack—a trail mix—to bring with you when you visit your own special place or places. While you can vary the mix based on what you like and have available, here is a basic recipe to get you started: Combine equal parts peanuts and/or any kind of nut you like (just be sure that you and whoever else will be eating the trail mix are not allergic to what you use), dried fruit (such as raisins, dried apricots, dates, figs, prunes), and chocolate candies (chocolate chips and/or M&M's® work nicely) in an unbreakable container or plastic bag. Carry it to your own special place and enjoy!

Related Reading

Other contemporary novels by Katherine Paterson

Come Sing, Jimmy Jo (1985)

Flip-Flop Girl (1994)

The Great Gilly Hopkins (1978)

Jacob Have I Loved (1980)

Park's Quest (1988)

The Same Stuff as Stars (2002)

Historical novels by Katherine Paterson

Jip: His Story (1996)

Lyddie (1991)

The Master Puppeteer (1975)

Of Nightingales That Weep (1974)

Preacher's Boy (1999)

Rebels of the Heavenly Kingdom (1983)

The Sign of the Chrysanthemum (1973)

Other

These books or series are stories Leslie shared with Jess in *Bridge to Terabithia:*

Chronicles of Narnia series by C. S. Lewis

Chronicles of Prydain series by Lloyd Alexander

Hamlet by William Shakespeare or

Hamlet for Kids (Shakespeare Can Be Fun series) by Lois Burdett

Moby-Dick by Herman Melville or
Moby-Dick (Great Illustrated Classics) by Herman Melville, retold by Shirley Bogart

These are two of the books Katherine Paterson read and enjoyed as a child:

The Secret Garden by Frances Hodgson Burnett
The Yearling by Marjorie Kinnan Rawlings

Bridge to Terabithia is also available on audiocassette.

Bibliography

Books

Paterson, Katherine. *Bridge to Terabithia.* New York: Crowell, 1977.

______. *The Invisible Child: On Reading and Writing Books for Children.* New York: Dutton, 2001.

______. *A Sense of Wonder: On Reading and Writing Books for Children.* New York: Plume, 1995.

Authors and Artists for Young Adults, Volume 31. Detroit: The Gale Group, 2000.

Meet the Authors. New York: Scholastic, 1995.

St. James Guide to Children's Writers, 5th ed. Detroit: St. James Press, 1999.

Something About the Author, Volume 133. Detroit: The Gale Group, 2002.

Newspapers and magazines

Horn Book Magazine, July/August 1990, Volume 66, Issue 4, pp. 412–424.

Horn Book Magazine, July/August 1993, Volume 69, Issue 4, p. 392.

Horn Book Magazine, November/December 1993, Volume 69, Issue 6, pp. 717–720.

Horn Book Magazine, July/August 1994, Volume 70, Issue 4, pp. 414–426.

The Reading Teacher, December 1994/January 1995, Volume 48, Number 4, pp. 308–309.

Web sites

Contemporary Authors Online, Gale 2002:
www.galenet.com

The Educational Paperback Association:
www.edupaperback.org/showauth.cfm?authid=66

Katherine Paterson's official Web site:
www.terabithia.com

Reading Rockets:
www.readingrockets.org/transcript.php?ID=12

Scholastic Author Studies Homepage:
www2.scholastic.com/teachers/authorsandbooks/authorstudies/authorhome.jhtml?authorID=80